A Sesame Street Passover

KIPPI AND THE MISSING MATZAH

קִיפִּי וְהַמַּצָּה הַחֲסֵרָה

By Louise Gikow
Illustrated by Tom Brannon

Random House New York

 Published in the United States by Random House Children's Books, a division of Random House, Inc., New York, in conjunction with Sesame Workshop. Originally published in slightly different form in the United States by Comet International, Inc., in cooperation with Sesame Workshop, in 1994.

Random House and the colophon are registered trademarks of Random House, Inc.

ISBN: 978-0-375-86126-0

MANUFACTURED IN CHINA 10 9 8 7 6 5 4 3

Elmo was very excited.

Spring was coming. His friend Kippi Ben Kippod — Kippi the Porcupine — was visiting him from Israel. And Kippi was making a Passover seder for all of his friends on Sesame Street!

As Elmo helped set the seder table, he sniffed happily. He could smell some wonderful smells coming from the kitchen. They were making him very hungry. Elmo couldn't wait for the guests to arrive.

Soon, the doorbell rang. When Elmo raced to open it, he found Big Bird standing there with Bert and Ernie.

"Happy Passover, Elmo!" Big Bird said.

"Happy Passover, Kippi!"

"Happy Passover!" echoed Bert and Ernie.

Then Prairie Dawn arrived with Cookie Monster. After them came Herry Monster with someone Elmo didn't know.

"This is my friend Zelda," said Herry. "She didn't have a seder to go to, so I brought her with me. Is that all right?"

"Of course it is, Herry," said Kippi. "Everyone is welcome at a seder! Come on in!"

Everyone stood around and admired the beautifully set table. Then it was time for the seder to start.

"Why doesn't everyone sit down?" Kippi asked. So everyone did.

"What is this blue book next to my plate, Kippi?" Big Bird asked. Everybody else had one, too.

"That's a Haggadah," Kippi explained. "It's the book that tells the story of Passover."

"What is Passover, anyway?" Herry wanted to know.

"Passover is a holiday that celebrates freedom," Kippi explained. "Many, many years ago, the Jewish people were slaves in ancient Egypt. The story of Passover is about how they became free people again. We tell that story every year at the seder. And we sing songs, and have a wonderful time!"

"What is a seder?" Prairie Dawn asked.

"It's the special meal that we eat on Passover," Kippi replied. "And all of these are seder foods. The matzah, for instance, is what the Jewish people ate when they left Egypt."

"Which is the matzah?" Prairie Dawn looked confused.

"It's right over there," Kippi said, looking at the table. Then he looked again. The plate that was supposed to hold the matzah was empty!

"Elmo!" Kippi said. "Where's the matzah?"

"Elmo doesn't know," said Elmo.

"Big Bird! Where's the matzah?"

"Don't ask me," said Big Bird. "I'm not even sure what matzah looks like!"

"It's something you eat," Kippi said. "It's flat, and crunchy, and looks a little like a big cracker. Has anybody seen it?" Nobody had.

"Elmo, did you put the matzah on the table?" Kippi asked.
"No," said Elmo. "Did Kippi?"
"No," said Kippi. "Maybe it's still in the kitchen!"
But it wasn't.

"Elmo must have dropped the matzah on the way back from the store," Elmo said sadly. Then he brightened. "Elmo will go find it!"

"I'll go with you, Elmo," said Kippi.

"We'll go too!" said Big Bird. "Maybe we can help!"

Outside, people hurried along Sesame Street. Some of them were heading to seders just like Kippi's. Old and young alike were gathering to celebrate the Passover holiday.

"We'll go this way," Big Bird told Elmo and Kippi.
"You go that way. Somebody is sure to find the matzah!"
"Good luck!" said Kippi.

Elmo and Kippi looked everywhere for the missing matzah. But it was nowhere to be found.

"What are we going to do?" asked Kippi worriedly. "We can't have the seder without matzah."

123

Just then, Elmo and Kippi heard a loud noise.
CRUNCH!
“What is that?” Kippi wondered.
“It sounds like it’s coming from Oscar’s can,” Elmo said.

Elmo knocked on the can. “Oscar?” he called.
“What?” came Oscar’s voice from inside.
CRUNCH!

Oscar popped his head out of his can.
And there, in his hand, was the missing matzah!

"That's it!" said Elmo. "Our matzah! Oscar found it!"

"Matzah?" said Oscar, chewing on a piece. "So that's what it is! Not bad. I bet it would be even better with some peanut butter and sardines . . . ." He bit off another piece. **CRUNCH!**

"Elmo needs it back," said Elmo. "We can't have our seder without matzah!"

"But I'm hungry," said Oscar. "And I like this matzah."

"Well, then," said Kippi. "I have an idea. Why don't you come to our seder? There's lots of food there."

"Food? What kind of food?" Oscar asked.

"Wait and see," said Kippi. "I think you'll like it."

So Elmo and Kippi took Oscar home with them.

When they got to Elmo's house, everyone else was already back.

"Did you have any luck?" Big Bird asked.

"Yes!" Elmo said. "We found the missing matzah!"

"Yaaay!" everyone cheered.

"So where's the food?" Oscar wanted to know.

"Here, Oscar!" said Elmo, taking something off the seder table. "Try some of this."

"What is it?" Oscar asked.

"Bitter herbs!" Kippi said.

"What are bitter herbs?" Oscar asked.

"A really yucchy tasting vegetable," Elmo explained.

"Bitter herbs are supposed to remind us of how bad it is not to be free," Kippi added.

Oscar opened his mouth.

"Be careful!" Kippi warned.

Then Oscar took a bite. First his eyes began to water. Then he sneezed, not once but four times.

"Powerful stuff!" he gasped. "These bitter herbs are all right."

"Here's something I think you'll like," Kippi said. "It's a sandwich of bitter herbs and matzah. That's one of the things we eat on Passover."

"Great idea," sniffled Oscar.

The seder was a great success. Everyone listened while Kippi told the Passover story, and then they all sang songs and ate the delicious dinner he had prepared.

Later on, as part of the holiday tradition, Kippi hid a piece of matzah somewhere in Elmo's house. It was like a treasure hunt: everybody had to look for it.

And who do you suppose found the missing matzah this time? Oscar again!

"Matzah, bitter herbs. . . pretty tasty," he admitted. "You know, Passover is a grouch's kind of holiday!"

Note to parents:

We hope that you and your family enjoy laughing, learning, and reading together as you follow the adventures of Elmo and Kippi in their search for the missing matzah. In our story, the Sesame Street Muppets learn about two essential Passover themes from their Israeli friend Kippi — the importance of inviting guests to a seder, and the fun custom of hiding a piece of matzah — the afikoman.

Below are descriptions of these and other concepts that appear in this book. We hope they enrich your understanding of the story, traditions, and customs of Passover.

Passover (פֶּסַח — Pesach): Passover is a holiday of freedom and birth — it recounts and celebrates the story of the Israelites' exodus from slavery in Egypt and the birth of a free Jewish people.

Seder (סֵדֶר — seder): The Hebrew word meaning "order," seder is also the name of the Passover celebratory meal at which the story is told of the Israelites' exodus from Egypt. The meal, as its name indicates, follows a set order. According to tradition, participants at the seder should feel as though they, themselves, were part of the Exodus. The foods, stories, and songs all serve to re-create and re-enact the story of the holiday.

Haggadah (הַגָּדָה — Haggadah): From the Hebrew word "telling," the Haggadah is the name for the book used at the seder that tells the story of the Exodus. In addition to providing the order of the evening meal, the Haggadah includes historical tales, legends, stories, prayers, and songs that help to recreate the Israelites' journey from slavery to freedom.

Matzah (מַצָּה — matzah): As Kippi describes, matzah is a thin, crunchy, cracker-like food that is eaten instead of bread during Passover. When the Israelites left Egypt, they packed their belongings and departed in a great hurry; they were afraid that Pharaoh (the Egyptian king) would change his mind and forbid them to go. In their haste, the Israelites did not have time to let their bread-dough rise. They packed the unrisen dough in their bags and carried it through the hot desert, where the sun baked it into hard, flat, crunchy cakes, called matzah. To remember the haste in which the Israelites fled Egypt, it is a tradition to eat matzah on Passover.

Bitter Herbs (מָרוֹר — maror): Usually a horseradish root or romaine lettuce, the bitter herbs are eaten to remind those at the seder of the hard and bitter lives the Israelites endured when they were slaves in ancient Egypt. They call to mind the fact that others still endure different forms of slavery today.

Hiding the Matzah: Early in the seder, a piece of matzah is broken in half. One half is left on the seder table and the other half — called the "afikoman" (the Greek word for dessert) — is put aside. Traditionally, the afikoman is the last food eaten at the seder. In some families, the leader of the seder hides the afikoman and the children try to find it — like a treasure hunt. If the children find the afikoman, they can re-hide it and demand a "ransom" for its return: after all, without the afikoman the seder cannot end. While there are many different traditions for "hiding the afikoman," its primary purpose is to involve the children as central participants in the seder, in a fun and engaging way.

Inviting Guests: On Passover, it is customary to invite guests to the seder — family, friends, or strangers, especially those in need. According to tradition, when the Israelites were slaves in ancient Egypt, they were considered "strangers" in the land. Inviting guests to the seder is a reminder of the past, and a continued commitment to be sensitive to others.